LOVEBIRDS

For Kim,

With gratitude.

LOVEBIRDS

STORIES

HANANAH ZAHEER

[signature]

BULL★CITY
PRESS

DURHAM, NORTH CAROLINA

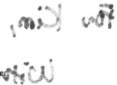

Lovebirds

Library of Congress Cataloging-in-Publication Data

Names: Zaheer, Hananah, 1977- author.
Title: Lovebirds : stories / Hananah Zaheer.
Identifiers: LCCN 2021037186 (print) | LCCN 2021037187 (ebook) | ISBN 9781949344257 (paperback) | ISBN 9781949344295 (ebook)
Subjects: LCSH: Families--Fiction. | BISAC: FICTION / Short Stories (single author). | FICTION / Literary. | FICTION / Family Life / Marriage & Divorce. | FICTION / Dystopian. | FICTION / Humorous / Black Humor. | LCGFT: Short stories.
Classification: LCC PS3626.A62523 L68 2021 (print) | LCC PS3626.A62523 (ebook) | DDC 813/.6--dc23
LC record available at https://lccn.loc.gov/2021037186
LC ebook record available at https://lccn.loc.gov/2021037187

This is a work of fiction. No identification with actual persons (living or deceased), places, buildings, and products is intended or should be inferred.

Published in the United States of America

Cover design: Savannah Bradley, with thanks to Stephanie Harris
Interior design: Spock and Associates

S P O C K
ASSOCIATES

Published by
BULL CITY PRESS
1217 Odyssey Drive
Durham, NC 27713
www.BullCityPress.com

CONTENTS

Father comes home from the Islamic Center on Friday and says too many women showed up.

"Looked like a funeral," he says and throws his keys on the console by the door. He frowns into mirror above it. There is a crack in the frame that he has been meaning to fix for days.

Mother goes on knitting whatever pink thing she is making these days. It is May and school is nearly out. Father sits down next to her and stretches his legs.

"It's vulgar, women coming to pray." Father doesn't like vulgar things. "No one did that at mosques back home."

He unlaces the black combat boots he wears everywhere. It's been twelve years since he left the Army, eleven since we left Pakistan.

Maybe we weren't who we thought we were, Mother likes to say.

Once a soldier always a soldier, Father likes to say, even when he is slicing meat behind the deli counter. He calls it muscle memory; a body remembers who you are even if you don't.

I don't want my muscles to remember, Mother always says in return. I want to forget.

She misses guavas off the tree in our front yard, the Azan waking her up, her mother's grave. Now she stops to study the stitches on the needle under the light of the lamp beside her, then resumes her knitting.

I turn the page on my Biology textbook. I am learning about meiosis and how a thing can become so many different, lesser, things.

"All that kneeling," Father says, "all that bending. It gives a man ideas."

"The women pray behind the men. If you can't see something, does it really matter?" I can hear the bitterness; her voice is ripe with it.

Father slowly peels a sock off his yellowed heel. "You can be bothered by a thing even if you can't see it." He drops the sock on the floor.

They make it sound like they are talking about religion, but I know what they mean: she, that he has stranded us in America; he, that she needs to stop blaming him for her loneliness.

She looks down at her hands. Despite the housework, they are beautiful: slender skeleton bound by skin. The needles pierce the pink holes over and over and I think I can see inside her, how the flesh moves across her bones, sliding, trapped in a perpetual motion. Above her neck, the jaw is clear, defined, pulsing. On her face, a flash of her old self, her heart in her eyes, pain and all. I wish she would let her fingers be still. Father asks if I am ready for exams.

He believes in education, he says, but I must put God first.

I nod. I like studying Biology and knowing that disorder is necessary for friction, that friction is necessary for heat, that heat breaks bonds. I like knowing how cells split, how that constant, quiet, violence gives life to the simplest of things: the universe, flowers, me. It comforts me, knowing that even God needs to break one thing to make another. Father goes to the bathroom and I hear the shower. We sit in the living room quietly, me on the floor and Mother on the sofa. I wonder what we should talk about.

"I am tired." I twist from side to side. "Want to go for a walk after dinner?"

She doesn't answer. In the hallway, the lightbulb flickers, then goes out.

"Someone will need to take care of that," she says and her hands keep moving.

The shower stops. Mother gets up to lay dinner on the table. She fills her time with chores. Everyone looks for things to hold themselves together.

I reach over to where she has left her knitting and slide one of the needles out. The empty loops keep their shape but I know the stitches will unravel at the first touch.

Father comes back, towel around his waist.

"What happened to the light?" A drop of water falls from the end of his beard onto my book.

I shrug and slide the needle up my sleeve. He misses the most obvious things.

"What's for dinner?" he asks. He keeps hoping for something new.

I close my book and go to his room. Every Friday night, Mother makes rice and chicken with cinnamon and cloves, like she did back home; he knows this. His shirt is on the bed. I hold the needle upright, in the middle. It looks like an arrow sticking out of a chest.

He is holding the bulb when I return with his clothes.

"Remember," he says. "If you don't fix things right away, they might become useless forever." He slides the shirt over his head. He is always saying things like this, but I don't agree with him anymore.

I bend to pick up my books, then remember what he had said about bending, and kneel instead. He looks at me and I try not to look away.

"Do you understand what I tell you?" He says this holding my gaze so steadily that I feel my heart char.

I nod. I don't say what I've learned: that the only way to fix a broken thing is by breaking it over and over until the fractures are so many that the first one becomes just that: the first.

He moves to the dining room and I follow. We sit, Mother and Father and I, and eat. I look at creases in Father's forehead and Mother's quick, unsettled fingers and wonder if the room feels as empty to them as it does to me. I hang my hand to my side and let the needle slide to my palm. I press it against my leg till it hurts. I like feeling. I could, I think, thrust it at my chest, my stomach, break through the skin to the chaos: the veins, the cells, the center of everything, to the parts that break and breathe and want. I could stab myself, over and over, until it matters, until I can no longer even moan. I clench my legs.

"Pray before you sleep," says Father. Mother spoons more rice onto my plate. We pretend we are whole.

LOVEBIRDS

None of her children have shown up for her birthday and Soraya sits at the window, watching the empty driveway, upright in the walnut wood chair that her father had ordered from the most expensive retailer in Lahore for her wedding—what was it, fifty years ago?—and ignores the hard-boiled egg and the orange and the glass of pomegranate juice on the tray in front of her, same tray she had used to carry soup and water to her mother she can't even remember how long ago, she thinks, feeling the burn from the heater on her small feet, and reaches for the single lovebird in the cage beside her—the silver coop her husband gave her on their twentieth anniversary complete with a blue bird and that sparkle in his eyes and a *Happy Anniversary, darling* even though it was the same year she had lost her mother and happy was the farthest thing from her mind but he had been feeling guilty, turned out, about his new, secret wife and his affections had become louder and more elaborate until all three kids had learned to say they wanted a love like their parents' and *Amma aren't you lucky* and her heart had fluttered at the sight of those delicate bird feet trembling on the perch, though later she had wondered if she really was lucky because that bird died in December and soon after it, her father was gone, too, and then her marriage when the letter from her husband's new wife arrived which, even now, is pressed into her old teaching copy of *Sense and Sensibility* on the bookshelf beside her, and which she had kept after all the deaths so that every time she stood in front of a classroom of eager girls, she could be reminded never to forgive her husband and to restrain the chirrups of the silly girls' hearts by telling them everything died at its most beautiful and it was best to believe only the words that slice the heart (truth was never meant to be kind) and now when her eyes spot that little blue edge that sticks out from between the pages, she holds the bird's neck gently between her knuckles and rubs her thumb against the red patch on its head nearly as soft as the hair on her daughters' heads when they were little, before they layered on hair color and rebellion and shaved and cut and changed entirely how they looked in an effort, she feels still, to rid themselves of her, and she was left with her son, the only one who had remained loyal—that sweet thing, sitting quietly by her bed day after day after her husband moved out, and who had wanted to give her his pocket money then, thinking it was that anniversary bird dying that had made her cry and cry and wrap her blankets around her as if she was building herself a cocoon— and who, though he comes to see her less and less, pays for her to keep her house now and who is across the city somewhere with a woman he has come to love more, just like his father; he was meant to sit in the chair beside her today, a good boy, looking out the window as she told him about all the dreams she had when she was a child, how she had wanted to train birds to deliver letters when she was young, how she wished her mother had warned her about endings, how she had given up the habit of looking forward and abandoned her yearly walk to the kitchen to hang the Scenes of Northern Pakistan calendar the maid and the cook so seemed to like and asked if he could find a new one for them, would he do that for her, and thinking of his absence, slowly her knuckles squeeze the small neck between them and with her other hand she holds the wings flapping strong and getting stronger—she knows they will be the strongest right before the end—until the claws scratching at her lap start to fail and she tells herself *this is just how life goes, Soraya, this is just how it is* and stares out the window. It is Tuesday, no Wednesday. Perhaps even Thursday. Tomorrow she will break off another small piece of gold from her wedding bracelets and ask the girl who brings her food to her to go to the market and buy another bird.

I had already been feverish for weeks when Husband came back from the neighborhood association meeting and said he had figured out what was wrong with me. There was a problem, he said. A big problem.

"That tree is poisoning you." He pointed at the willow's crown visible beyond our gate. "We have to cut it down."

The tree was in the middle of the neighborhood park, the only place I went besides visiting other women who lived on our street. It was a relief from my days which had been downy and unspoiled at the beginning of my marriage, but lately had taken on a rotting quality. I found my limbs drained of life. My saliva always tasted like ash. More and more it became difficult to let Husband touch me. I had taken to sneaking out to the park in the afternoons when he was at work and his parents were sleeping. I liked hiding behind the curtain of leaves, my back against the sturdy trunk, pulling my shalwar up to feel the air lick the hair on my legs. I liked how the wind set the leaves in motion, how they shivered. Sometimes, when no one was looking, I pulled my shirt up and rubbed my stomach against the roots. I was doing this nearly every day by then, rushing through housework so I could escape outside.

What do you even do there, Husband would ask me, even though I knew he had followed me once or twice. Rest, I would say, and my face would burn in memory of the willow's skin against it. The tree had become my excitement.

I hated the idea of what my life would look like without the willow. Husband had already objected to the book club, morning tea at the Fairweather Hotel, and monthly visits to my sister's house.

Association rules, he said. If we choose to live in a neighborhood like this, we had to follow the rules.

It was just like him to try to take away the only thing I did without his permission. I would rather he cut me down than the tree.

"A tree can't be poison," I said, not meeting his eyes. "It's just a tree."

A lot of other men were worried, too, he said. Their women were going for walks in the morning, evening. They were lingering by the tree, clustering under its branches. Had I suggested the idea to them?

I had, of course. If we stayed inside our homes, we would wilt. Fresh air and exercise was necessary for us to grow, we told each other.

"I think...well..." Husband waited by the dining table so I could pull out the chair for him. "Do you hear any sounds when you sit under it, any whispers? Do you feel...unusual?"

"What kind of unusual?" I asked and heaped a spoonful of the cardamom rice I had just finished making on his plate. Husband's mother had said it would help her son become tender, add fragrance to his skin, maybe help my body accept him easier. It concerned everyone that I did not want to have a child.

"Strange things have been happening," he said.

First it was Fatgirl who worked at the bank and refused to get married when her father brought home the man from America, maybe a restaurant owner, maybe a businessman, something to do with food, but American. Then Babyface and her younger sister showed up without their hijabs on a billboard for Popstar Idol down on Alam Road and all us neighbors stood in our yards to listen to their father shouting before we ran inside to turn the TV on. Then old Doctor Uncle's young wife asked him for a divorce, saying he couldn't function in the bedroom and she was not going to wait around for him to die. Lawyer's wife refused to do anything she was told to do: the dishes sat on the table with chicken bones drying on them for hours, the laundry had started to pile up, she left the house whenever she wanted and she started wearing perfume that made her smell like roses at nighttime.

"I think...the men think... there are Jinns in the trees," Husband said and looked very worried. "They're stealing your thoughts. They are deforming your mind, making women think you don't need your men to live." He creased his brow, then turned his mouth into a pucker. "Even trees don't grow without seeds," he said.

"Eat something," I said.

I thought the rice might distract him. Husband's mother was always feeding him away from his anger. He picked a cardamom seed off the spoon and took a big bite. I tried not to think of the feel of his starchy mouth on mine, him trying to push himself into my body. This is what you want, he would say. You want a child, he would say.

One chew and a grunt and Husband opened his mouth wide again. His tongue rolled the rice back out. The grains glistened, and a single one hung on to a strand of his saliva.

"Too much salt," he said and wiped the taste off on the back of his hand. The grain fell.

"In the tree?" I asked, thinking of running my tongue across the ragged willow bark, tasting the wood, sucking on a red, swollen catkin.

Husband pushed the plate away. "I hope you won't talk nonsense once you're a mother," he said.

Husband was sad about cutting the tree. When he was young and the roots of the tree were beginning to run tracks in the dirt, he used to play by it. He and his friends hung on the slender limbs and carved their names on the trunk. They burned the tips of feather-veined leaves with cigarettes. They pissed on the roots under each other's feet.

"The tree watched me grow into a man," Husband said. "But it's old now, I guess."

I told him I would stop going to the park. I didn't mean it, but I thought I had to do what I could to change his mind.

"You don't have to cut it down," I said. "Think of all your own memories."

It saddened me to know the willow was out there, soaking in the sun, swaying gently in the breeze. It had no idea of what was coming for it.

"Don't let your imagination ruin something you love," I said.

Husband shook his head and dropped his shoulders till his chest was a hollow, and when he said, "You have to cut down even your friends if they rot," I knew he was feeling betrayed.

The next day Uglygirl's father and Grandfather and uncle and brother gathered at the park with axes and swords.

"No machines," Husband said, when he was leaving to join them. "They might scare the Jinns away."

The line of men wearing determined faces stretched all the way past our house, round the roundabout, and down into the mosque. They took turns at the axe. All morning, I could hear the grunts of the men and the thwack, thwack, thwack of the blade slicing the wood. Husband came home for lunch and said that behind the sweep of leaves, the trunk was a thing of horror. Hundreds of clusters of red sprout, the size of eyes. The middle swollen, pregnant with ants that had poured out and bit his hand.

"The Jinns are fighting back," he said. "Stay indoors."

I was watching from my balcony when the tree buckled. All down the street, I could feel the women on their own balconies wince when the axe blade sliced its final arc into the heartwood. The willow arched and fell, branches reaching across the grass. The crown covered the park gate straight across. I tried to swallow the knot in my throat.
The men hollered and wiped their brows; the day had been heavy. They were warriors, weary and filled with elation. They kneeled against the stump and turned their chests to the sun.

Praise Allah, I imagined them saying. We have saved our women.

Behind them, on the naked stump, sap glistened. They rubbed it on their fingertips and brought the scent to their noses.

Fresh cut, they might have said. Now watch the butterflies die on it.

The next morning, I woke up early to Husband talking loudly on the phone.

"Your dead father," he snapped, when I asked him who it was. Then he threw on his shirt and pants and ran down the stairs. From the balcony, I could see other men moving toward the park, too. The morning mist had not yet fully cleared and they looked like shadow bodies slowly coming into being. I could make out Babyface on her balcony next door.

"What's going on?" I asked.

"The sap," she said, pouting in the same way she did in magazines and on billboards. "Baba said the tree is oozing something awful. Smells like peppermint blood. Can't you smell it?"

I shook my head but my heart came alive then. That was nothing like the willow had ever smelled to me. I leaned over the railing as far as I could. The men were scattered near the roots, amidst remnants of branches. Dark amber bled from the stump and pooled around their feet. Some men stood at a distance and looked at it. Husband took a few steps closer and then said something to the others.

It's the blood of the Jinns, I could imagine him saying. We were right. Look at the bastards bleeding. We cut their heads off.

He lifted his foot and looked at the bottom of his shoe. I could see it took him an effort to lift the knee, like the earth was pulling at him. The sap was attaching to his soles. The tree was angry; it knew what had happened to it. I was filled with elation. It knew. It knew. My body celebrated. I swayed back and forth against the railing. I wanted to scream and cry and laugh. I wanted to fall off and fly into the air. I wanted to lay myself on the sap, cover my arms with the amber, fill my mouth with the color. I wondered if it was warm or cold. I wondered if it would make my jaw clench.

Then I heard a shout.

"I'm stuck," Husband yelled. Next to him, Uglygirl's father fell. It looked as if something had pulled him down. There was a commotion and then suddenly all the men were yelling and making noises. None of them could move.

"What's happening?" I called out to Husband, but my voice was not loud enough to cut through the noise.

When the haze lifted some, I could see that the ooze from the willow stump was no longer a trickle. It poured thickly and came up around the men's shins. They were stuck, trapped in the amber liquid. Their cries, which at first had sounded surprised, had become angry and they tried to shovel the sap away with their hands. But there was no stopping the tree. The sap poured heavier and heavier and when it got a hold of the men's knees and moved up their thighs, they became afraid. They called out to us.

"I can't move," Husband said over and over. "Help," he yelled. "Help."

I looked down the street. All the neighborhood balconies were filled with women. We called out to each other.

"They are getting swallowed," Fatgirl said.

Lawyer's wife asked if we should do something.

"I don't know," I said. "Husband said to stay inside."

In the park, the sap kept rising. When the mist started to burn off, we saw that the men were no longer fighting. By the time the sun was high in the sky, their bodies were covered completely and our men were nearly relics trapped in giant amber catkins, petrified with their fears and their anger. The willow had swallowed their cries.

WEDNESDAY

It's late on Wednesday again. He stands before the wreckage of his house, the smoke burning a fire track inside his chest. A commotion around him: firefighters and water and neighbors with cell phones held out to capture the sight. Everyone studies the rubble. *That's the husband.*

The air is scorched wood and curtain and carpet and burnt flesh. His stomach has become used to this smell, to the ripe, seared skin, the char of bones. It came just past Isha prayer, as it does every night, with smoke that travels in from the East and descends into the smoldering beams of the roof, lighting up the night sky. A sizzle. Water bursts back into the fireman's hose and pieces of the terrace where she had stood just hours earlier, heave upward. The bedroom window swallows the flames.

The firefighters return to their truck. The neighbor goes back to his own window, his wife next to him, a phone to his ear. A beam rises from the flames and settles itself back into the walls, repaired. Little embers fly.

Hellfire spit, he thinks, as he does every evening.

It could almost be beautiful, this coming back together of his house, his life. It was what he had believed a long time ago, when the fights still felt like love. He had believed he could always fix things, reverse the damage: ruin to restoration. He could almost believe it now; almost, except he knows: the day will reverse into the same peaceful morning and by the evening all will be up in flames again.

He thinks he can hear her, sharp and scared, amid the angry pieces of ash that sigh as they float up from the ground. It makes him sick. He never could stand her loud. And she was loud, everywhere:

in laughs, in opinions, in their bed. He wants to cover his ears but he always finds himself unable. Recovery is always ugly.

It's late afternoon now. Soon the sun will retreat into the morning and he will be inside lying on the bed next to her. She will walk in from the bathroom, toothbrush in hand, and she will ask him the same question he has been trying to answer forever now: *Would you kill me if you thought no one could find out?* He buries his hands inside his pockets and shivers.

In peaceful days she would call it a window-day, sitting in a chair with a book and a cigarette and leaning her head back to absorb the sun. *That is what this feels like.* She would point at the light. Even now, above the smolder, the sky is clear, the kind of clear blue that stirs in him a want to soar, to inhale the expanse. It was the same feeling he had the first time they touched. That had been a Wednesday, too. It had tasted of possibility.

He looks at the bedroom window upstairs. The fire glow has dimmed and it makes him a little sad, finding himself alone in the flower bed outside.

Downstairs, he imagines, the varnish on the new dining table is starting to heal.

At sunset, they were always able to hear the call for prayer from the mosque down the street. Neither of them cared to pray much, but long before the first time she had walked back in from the balcony and laughed at seeing him trying, hard, to find himself in devotion, they had liked making love to it.

He sweats now even though the heat is receding and the morning is rolling in thick and chilly. Soon he will find himself back in his bed and the day will start again. He will fall asleep for just a little while and when she asks him the question, he will pull her onto him and find her mouth. It will almost make him forget. Almost.

That it had been dark, another half hour to go before sunset, before the city grid turned on the electricity again. She had not liked his answer; the kisses, the tremble of his voice saying *you are so hot you drive me crazy*, the afternoon in bed. She had stood by the balcony door, naked, holding her hand above the flame of a candle, watching him pray. She had looked cold.

You are always trying, she had said.

He had reached over and released the gas in the fireplace. She shouldn't have been outside. Not in this weather, not at this time, not where anyone could see.

I don't need that.

She could always make him twist, double over, forget himself. This he already knew but it surprised him how quickly his anger had erupted this time, poured out, he felt, from every inch of his skin.

He remembers dragging her across the room. He remembers her defiant face. He remembers calling her a whore. He remembers her saying she hates him. He remembers wanting to fuck her, he remembers her biting his lip. He remembers thinking the neighbors would hear. He remembers leaving the room.

He doesn't remember what set everything on fire.

The blast behind him is always muted, like a body falling on a wooden floor, a thud. He stood in the hallway until flames leapt out of the bedroom door and licked at him. He had not known a blaze could sweep everything away so quickly, the heat so alive it almost made him want to swim in its tendrils. Almost. He had almost run back for her.

He can't help but be afraid, even now. It's her face, mostly. Every day, he sees that look on her face when she runs at the door. Hair trailing her face, everything ablaze. And her cry. He is always surprised at how unafraid she looks, even as she burns. He always wants to get away.

GOD IN THE CHICKEN COOP

I wanted to see God, and he said he would show Him to me. What God was doing in the chicken coop behind our house, I never knew. But we huddled in there, praying for it, skin against skin, hand against new breasts, mouth inside a mouth. We stayed, sometimes all afternoon, me blinking, trying to breathe, holding still until the simmering, slow panting of the Lahore summers grew so loud that I worried I would not hear Him. That's it, he would say. You will see, you just have to look. And I did, through the wires in the small skylight, meant to give the chickens the illusion of freedom. I saw it in the sparkle of clouds moving above the minaret of the mosque down the street, in the stillness of the treetops, new with budding flowers. Somewhere in the midst of the fluttering, the noise, the chickens, I think, saw it too. They calmed their desperate slams against the wall, stopped the pecking, searching for sustenance, and looked up at the sky and were still.

A RECORD OF HER MONTHS

By November, deep into the medicinal haze, she won't know why she picked up the dead sparrow from beneath the park bench, though mostly, they will tell her she couldn't resist the delicate shrivel, the curling claws. It reminded her of her daughter's hand, they will say, too blue, too stiff inside the coffin. Perhaps, like her daughter, she had wanted to have a box of odd objects, treasures from around the garden. She won't remember now, strapped to her bed, the tip of a needle kissing her wrist. Soon, oblivion. Then, she will dream of the park where she could breathe, where her daughter laughed, all the way back in that lifetime that was August.

In August, there were two months: the one that was filled with buying cotton wool for a school project and taking her daughter to Anarkali Bazaar for yellow and green bangles and insisting on a stop at Liberty Market for pomegranate juice and telling her daughter *have an ice cream, little bird* and the Saturday trips to the New and Old bookshop for a magazine for her, a chapter book for her kid even if it cost more money than her husband allowed. And then the other month, the one where she picked out the smallest shroud she could find and washed between her daughter's toes and sat alone at her kitchen table, a packet of oatmeal in her hands, crying because she had no one to make it for. Between the two months was that single turn from Alam Avenue onto Ghalib Road, that single moment of failure. Her husband was right. He had told her not to drive, hadn't he?

In September, she tucked the bird inside her shirt and took it up to her room. It looked so small, so helpless it broke her heart. She tore up a pillowcase and made a pouch for it. When her husband sat across from her and asked if there was anything on her mind, she thought *no, but I have something on my body*. It was a comfort to have a secret. She liked the feel of the bird under her shirt as she walked about her house. At night, she laid it on the pillow next to her and pretended that it was alive. When she cried, she used the head to wipe her eyes. But then, it started smelling. Her husband told her to get away from him. The doctor came to find out why she smelled like rot. When they took the bird away, she sobbed; fell to the floor and did not hear her husband call her a *disgrace to my house.*

In October, she tried to escape: the gate, ladder and over the back wall of the hospital. The first time, the nurses understood and told her to quit it. The second time, they limited her hours outside. The third, they called her husband. He wrote. He had hoped some time away would fix her but now he was done. He had no patience for what she had become. *Why would she do this to him? Why couldn't she just be normal? Why wouldn't she let people help?* Why, why, why? The questioning was persistent. Someone left a dead mouse at her door one night. Giggles trailed her movement from bathroom to dining hall to her room.

I like dead things, I guess, she said one day. *I guess I like that things die.* No one liked that answer.

APARTMENT

That summer they had almost given up. They went to work and came back in the early evening. They made dinner quietly and politely asked how each other's day was. They watched TV. Sometimes, he fell asleep on the sofa and she left him there and went to bed alone. On weekends they went to the secondhand market down on Liberty Road and rummaged through piles of other people's discards. Snowshoes and teacups and old sports trophies and plaques and sweaters that said *Made in USA*. She liked to look for things that told a story, and he picked things he thought might be useful. Sometimes, they found something really unusual, like a half-written diary, and then they laughed over it, momentarily excited, but that feeling always passed.

In this way, their apartment was becoming a museum of rejection. They spent a long time setting it up with their finds, putting a thing here, then there, then taking it away altogether and abandoning it in the hallway closet for later. They would start in one room, each standing in front of the wall, each with a hammer in hand. He avoided touching her, waiting until she picked from the sack of discards in the center of the room, then reached in; she walked back and forth quietly, talking under her breath, unaware of him. She was faster to decide where to hammer or tape or hang and moved quickly. First one wall, then another, then the floor, then the side table. She strung fairy lights and yarn between windows, wrapped their lengths around shelves, draped the neck of the lightbulb. Sometimes, she lost interest and left the ends hanging. Her part of the room looked wild, like half-told anecdotes. He considered his decisions. He asked himself whether a thing belonged with another thing. He debated whether it was more important to admire something from a distance or to be able to reach it in case he needed to. When he was done, he packed away the hammers and cleared the nails off the ground. By the time he made it out of the first room, she would be sitting on the sofa, sipping water slowly, her eyes on the TV. He knew he should probably say something at the time, something like *good, better, best, you must never let it rest* or something else like that which would made her laugh burst through the room like when they had first moved in. But between the stacks of secondhand magazines and old phones and batiks from Indonesia or Malaysia—they hadn't been able to agree which—they had filled their walls with other people's lives. There was no room left for her laugh to echo. Thinking this, he could never bring himself to speak. Usually, he walked past her to the kitchen and poured himself a glass of water and stood there drinking it till it was empty. Then he wiped the countertop with his hand even though there was usually nothing there to clean.

Once, from the corner of his eye, he saw her smiling at a ceramic plate she was holding up to the wall. She was standing next to the window in their bedroom, and the sunlight was falling on her face. It lit up the small mole beside her eye. He watched her lean in close, her nose nearly touching the porcelain like she was smelling it. Then, she turned her face gently and closed her eyes, her cheek resting against the plate. He wanted to ask what it was that was making her smile this way. But he had not seen this kind of tenderness on her face for a very long time and thinking that she must be savoring the feeling, he said nothing.

Standing in the room, looking at her next to the window, he could remember the time when they had looked at the bare walls and said *we should do something about this*. He had been just as full of love, then. The room had been just as bright.

There is a tornado coming to Pennsylvania. I think they said Wednesday on TV. Or could have been "When is the day?" I couldn't exactly tell because I was in the kitchen making Abba's dinner, and his oxygen machine, eight years old, huffed and puffed and made such a racket, you woulda thought it was the thing with the cancer in it, and not the man.

Now that he's gone, I am laying claim to his Red '66 Mustang and getting out of here before the storm hits. I have never been much into cars, but Sara called after the funeral this morning and said she wanted to take a look at Abba's things and that the car was hers, Abba had said so. I couldn't think of any good reason why she should have it, given that she couldn't even bother coming to say goodbye to our father, or for the eight years before this; it seemed like she and her New York suits just didn't want to be seen around Erie. She no longer had the right.

So I said that, to which she said, "Why are you so hateful?" and to which I said, "Are you jealous Abba loved me better?"

The older sister in her was prickling, I could tell, so I told her the car wasn't worth much anymore anyway—the guys who had come to fix up the house, before I put it on the market, had spilled paint on it.

She got so mad, I could tell the vein in the middle of her forehead was popping out, a spitting image of Abba's temper.

"How could you let it happen? You were in charge." She was right about that.

The day before he passed, I took his money from the bank. Then, in the midst of him throwing the bowl of soup against the wall, telling me he didn't like seeing my face just like he didn't like seeing my mother's, I dragged everything from the house onto the driveway, called a truck to pick up the lot, hung my favorite air freshener around the car's rearview mirror, folded maps in the glove compartment. I scrubbed the house clean top to bottom, scoured the old walls where his machine was plugged in, until my knuckles were raw and the water dripped well and good into the socket.

Even the man who came to pick up the hospital bed, the broken machine, was impressed at how organized I was. Smiled at me from behind his mustache and complimented me on how well I had kept dad's medical records, recorded every meal and everything. He looked down my shirt and said any man would be lucky to have me around. I could have settled for him, maybe, could have seen myself in a life, if he hadn't asked me about my sister, and didn't she and him go to high school together? And had I really lived in this house all my life? It's a big world out there, he said.

Now, the trunk sat open waiting for me load my suitcase. I had to go. So I told Sara I was very sad, and had been for years, and now that the everything was sold off, and I no longer had a home, I needed time to myself. I needed to find a purpose.

So of course she said she was coming, this is what sisters were for, and wait, hold on, had I put the house on the market when Abba was still alive?

And I was silent.

And she was too, and I knew she was chewing on her nails, turning thoughts over in her head.

She said, slowly, again. "When did you put the house up for sale, Mona?"

And when she put my name out there like that, I knew she was starting to understand. So said I don't remember, but I had to go.

And she told me I better not go anywhere; we had to talk about this.

And I said, sure. I'll wait for you at the house, and dragged my suitcase from the living room to the garage.

I mean it, she said.

And I said okay.

Because it was, everything was finally okay, the sickness was gone, and the caretaker job out west was mine. And the only thing left between her and me was a few years spent lying together in the same room at night, listening to my mother crying when my father's cancer was discovered, and the silence after she left.

There was no way to tell her that by the time she finds me, I will have scraped paint from the car, grime from the walls, and taken off to outrun a tornado somewhere else.

THINGS I SAY TO MY SON WHILE HE SLEEPS

If you end up breaking your promise and climbing out the window into the alley and meeting those boys whose beards are nearing manhood and whose angry eyes pick at my body—I know they see a useless woman, a crumbling moral life, no man to protect me—and who slip you into the dark mouth of the old internet café down in Johar Town and who won't let you smoke (though I am grateful to them for this), with whom your eyes sharpen when you tell them you want to be pure and when they pat your shoulders and say *you are doing Allah's work, brother*, and who give you advice on how to bow when you pray and hand you a gun and tell you your father is probably in Hell, though listen he was a good man, no matter what he did— it is not a sin to work at a bookstore when you have four mouths to feed, even when the books have things that are shameful and you have to listen, he was not spreading immorality, son, he was keeping you alive—if they find you battles to fight, tell you all the things wrong with the doctor's family you've lived next door to your entire life, whose mother carried you when you were little, whose children you played with, who was the first to run to your father with when he lay bleeding in the street (remember, he steadied your hand over your father's chest, showed you how to keep the blood inside?)—but whose daughter steps out of her house without covering her head and if little fires of shame burn inside you for knowing them and because you see my head uncovered in the market, too, and those boys tell you that the entire neighborhood is watching you share your wall with a Kafir, that your father died not because of the bullet but because he *was* sin and because an unholy hand touched him at the end, and if they burn enough of your heart that it scatters like cinder and if you find yourself bold, in the moonlight, and your feet are steady on the brick along our street and, even before the chimney smoke has died down in our house, even before your brothers have gone to sleep, already you can feel yourself a man, the kind of man who wants to clean all the sin from his blood, who will be wrapped in coldness at the kitchen table in the morning, the kind of man who will always find purpose in erasure, who tells himself he will never bear the insult of a blasphemer's existence on Allah's earth, if those boys' words are the beat of your steps, if your hand is bold enough to ring the doorbell, knowing I am waiting for you just a few feet away, knowing your brothers are looking for you like you used to look for your father, and if you stand at that door, waiting for it to open, and if your fingers are just a little numb around the gun and if you shift your feet and if you feel as if there a million eyes on your back but you feel alive, more alive than you have ever felt, forgetting that your existence *is* the purest thing there can be, turn the gun to your own head, son, and shoot.

The first time I see the girl, she is standing at the bottom of a coal pile across from the harvest tent, soot face, scared eyes. It is winter and I am holding my boy in the sun. He needs daylight, water, a burning fire at night. He needs new insides, too, but for now it's all I can to keep him living.

"I'm not doing anything wrong," she says. "I'm only eating carbon."

The front of her dress is a lumpy pouch. Her mouth drips crumbs. One side of her face is melted, birth melted, sadness melted. I sit my son on the ground. He has trouble walking lately but he loves the earth against his skin. I stretch my burning arms.

"Where did you hear about carbon?" I ask.

Our books became ash, then dust, years ago. The girl looks a little younger than my son, maybe ten, not old enough to remember books, schools, our lives before this life. I can hardly remember what came before. Before hurts so bad it's not even a memory. My recollection begins at holding my son against my chest on the ride from the city to the mines, his body still, mine shivering. *Illegal*, the stamp on my wrist said. That's all I can remember.

"My father," she says. "He says it's what we need to live. He says everything is made of carbon." She points a finger at my son, then me. "You fix people."

I nod. I try. In my previous life I was a nurse, on hire as companion for old people whose families had no time to comfort them until their deaths. Now, people come to me with broken bones and open wounds.

At first, they offered me small things—an old brooch, leftover coins, a piece of cloth—in exchange for relief. I tried; I bandaged arms, held sobbing frames. Then their possessions, and my comfort, ran out. I started feeding them coal. Ground up, in water, on their tongues. I was feeding them relief, really. It made them return, over and over. Pain is a difficult thing to cure. It's important they keep believing.

"I used to be a doctor," I say. "I know how."

My son smiles up at me. He believes it, too, knows I'm the only thing keeping him from the ditch over by the edge of the colony. The others know I'm different. I can ask Truck Man for things they need: medicine and bandages and sometimes poison. People are grateful to me. Grateful will burn the fire in your stove. Grateful will make people spit their kidneys out for you.

"I need this for my father," she says. "He says he's made of it, too."

"Your father's right," I say. "But carbon isn't free."

The girl is eating our winter reserves. Out here in the colony, we need fire, we need heat. If I want my son to see March, I have to pay the Truck Man well. In September, he brought me supplies, new tools, took the last harvest back to some hospital in the city, to some antiseptic hallways where only the chosen ones still live. But the hunger is growing, out there and in here. The rows of potatoes and daikons behind our tent are dying. Not enough nutrition left in their weak bodies. My son needs sustenance, some meat. I need more harvest.

Last week, Truck Man came with urgent requests. *Two kidneys, now. No, make it seven. Or no medicine for your son.* I have to do what I can.

"Where are your parents?" I unhook a flask from my waist, hand it to my son. Two sips. I take it back and turn the cap even though my own mouth needs relief. I'll drink water tomorrow. Two days for him, one for me. I would do anything for my child.

"My father's sick," she says. "Working."

I nod. Both things are possible. Back in the city, in our homes, we were people. Out here, we are rats between barbed wires. We have forgotten how to live. Dig, dig, dig for coal all day. Lift, lift, lift on trucks in the evening. Now, it's the day and the earth and the sky and the wind trying to dry or squeeze or suck or burn the life out of us.

The minutes are slow, the minds empty. I'm the only one who still remembers we have bodies. I'm the only one who has to.

"Your mother?"

Her fingers find her mouth. "She lives somewhere else." She fishes out black and watches it drip onto her feet. "My father said she likes where she is."

I hear the quiver. That's all I need.

"I can heal your father," I say. "So he can stay with you."

She looks fertile enough, considering. Nothing broken, voice still strong. Her skin has vigor.

She nods. "He says his heart is broken."

A new truckload of people arrived in July. New sicknesses, new fears. I listened and I harvested, sometimes the same bodies twice. One woman lasted for days after. That's determination: the mind disbelieved long after the body knew what happened, hung on, hoping. Hope makes people come to me. Now winter's next door and everyone's carrying worry. Their blankets are barely thread. No one's got time to feel better. Maybe their spirits are breaking. My tent's been empty.

"I can heal your father," I say. The wind whips my ankles. "For a small price."

She bites her lip, looks at the pile of coal. I wait. Children take their time to trust; they know better.

"I don't have anything to pay." She is unsure but I know already; we have made a bargain.

I bend to lift my son to standing. "I have to put him to bed first."

"He doesn't look good." She says. Straight, knocks the air out of my lungs. "You could give him carbon."

I nod. I can comfort her, I can send a piece of her to save somebody in the city. I can keep this balance. But I can do nothing about my son dying.

His head is light against my chest. He smells like dirt, or nothing.

He was beautiful once, raindrop eyes and sapling skin. Now, he is bone and hide. When he sleeps, I can see his heart. Thump, space, thump under the ribs. I kiss his hair. Just one more winter, then I can let him go.

"Okay," I say. "That tent, five minutes. And then everything will be fine."

On Tuesday, I finally meet him.

He comes into the post office where I work, steps up to the counter and says he received a phone call telling him there was a package. Tony, who is at the corral next to mine, chomps on his dentures, looks him up and down.

"Here, sir, I called you." I wave him over, ignore the bitter gourd face Tony is making. He is old and vicious and keeps saying it's too bad my mother didn't teach me what it was really like to be a good woman.

The man walks up to me.

"A package?" he asks, and then, "Is there some problem?"

I consider giving him the kind of bullshit I give other men, something like *your name was flagged by the head office, or security reasons, terrorism.* I pretend to look at my computer.

"Name?" I make him spell it out, even though I know who he is. He's been sending letters to the same address. They always come back, *return to sender* across the front. I know the handwriting by now: the careless, angry cursive of a petty woman. He seems devoted, despite the rejection. This is the first package she's sent.

I shuffle some papers. "You send a lot of letters to this address."

He gives me a how-did-you-know look.

I nod. "We have to keep an eye out."

Sweat rolls down my front. I wonder if he can see down the unbuttoned *V* of my shirt. I can feel Tony's stare burning into the side of my face.

"The package?" The man raises his eyebrows.

"Yes, the package." I pretend to study the papers. "Aha! I'll be right back."

Tony follows me into the back.

"That guy looks like a sissy." I ignore him. He is angry because I said no to Atlantic City with him. Just because he put his fingers inside me in the breakroom once doesn't mean I am going to let him do it forever.

"He is too good for you." Tony shuffles around to where he can see my face. "Everyone is."

He smells sweaty, even his eyelids are moist. He looks like my father telling my mother to sit up, eat. The room heats up real sudden. Bastard. He just wants to see me cry.

I return to the counter. The package is wrapped neatly. His name is across the front, same as the last three envelopes.

"Here." I put the box on the counter.

His mouth twitches. His fingers are long—I imagine he would be careful lifting a piece of cake to his mouth, cutting another to feed me. I'll have to find my mother's recipes. By the time she killed herself, both of us were too sad to make anything nice to eat.

"You can open it here. If you want," I say.

He lifts his fingers to his mouth. His forehead creases. I can see him trying to decide. I want to tell him that I understand. Boxes like this carry loneliness. It's hard to look at the leftovers of a life, to remember you felt safer. I find a box cutter under the table.

He slices the tape. I watch the skin on the back of his knuckles. He seems thoughtful, an attentive man. The kind of man who would tape up your mirror if you broke it against your forehead, who would stick around to clean up the shards. He doesn't seem like the kind of man who would give up. I think I might like to lick the insides of his knee.

"Must be nice to get gifts." I say.

"It's from my mother." He laughs, digs inside the box, and pulls out a dirty bird cage.

"My mother used to give me gifts," I say. "Mostly old things around the house that she wrapped in newspapers. She was crazy."

He pulls out some books, an old calendar with dates crossed off.

"My mother, too," he says, and I can see he is embarrassed.

"I can clean it for you." My leg is shaking, fast, under my desk.

The line is building.

"Sorry about your mother," he says.

"Neeeext." Tony's loud.

He closes up the box. "Thank you."

"That's a nice cage." I press the box cutter against my wrist.

"Thanks." He smiles and walks away and the man next in line is already at my counter saying *stamps*. His face blurs in front of me and I can hear the phlegm rattling in Tony's throat.

I reach under my table for the stamps and then before I know it, I am standing up on my chair and saying, "Hey, can I have that?"

He is at the door. He turns and looks at me. Everyone else does too, and behind me I hear Tony saying, "Unbelievable. Just unbelievable."

He walks back and puts the box on the counter.

"Sure," he says. "Keep it all."

I know I shouldn't. But maybe if I tell him that that I love way he writes, he might like it. He might like that sometimes I put his letters inside my shirt and wear them till they are soaked with sweat; he might get it. It might be better than Atlantic City.

"I can play the piano," I say.

"Stop," he says.

I can feel want gathering in my skin. It is painful.

"I can bake."

"Stop," he says, louder.

"I can write you letters."

"Jesus." Tony yells. "Your arm."

I look. There's a neat, fresh, cut. I'm dripping on stamps.

"I'm sorry," I say and I mean it and I want him to stay. "I'm sorry."

But his eyes have darkened. And the room is darkening. And I can hear Tony saying *Jesus Christ* over and over and before I know it, he is gone and the lid has closed on me.

It was the road trip that she had been talking about taking for a while. Was it to see her mother, I had asked her, and she had stared at the soapy floor and said she couldn't wait to drive off into the mountains. So, when she came to the car wash, her smile hiding behind dark sunglasses and a somber mouth, and said she was finally going, I knew I had to be the one to take her. She cocked her head to the side as if she was trying to read me, and I just continued wiping down the car window, the water suddenly raising goosebumps on my arms, and she shrugged and said okay, that would be fine.

The next morning, my '82 Chevy Celebrity cleaned and waxed, I pulled up to her house, nine minutes and thirty-two seconds away from mine, a brown brick one story with red shutters, pink tricycle on the front lawn, and a door lock that was impossible to open with a credit card. I came with nothing but the clothes on my back. She ran out, a flash of light in the dark, slipped a cardboard box into the trunk and without a backward glance, told me to go, go, go. I asked her why she had brought her things; that hadn't been the plan, not the way fresh starts happen. And she told me to mind my business and that just because she had agreed to a ride did not mean I could ask her questions. And because her eyes nailed mine with a wild expectation, a crazed freedom that set my heart racing, I drove.

She was quiet as we left Baltimore in our rearview mirror, texting on her phone all through Pennsylvania, and finally when we entered Ohio, I asked her what her mother was like, how long it had been since they met.

She frowned, deep creases in her forehead I have never noticed before, and said what about being a mother?

I repeated the question and she laughed, the creases receding, and said oh *her* mother, her *mother*, was fine, decent enough.

I didn't know what was funny because she had always said some women leave because they just aren't able to be mothers, and I had understood that, about being unwanted, about the weight of that discontent. It had been clear that this was the link she was building between us, this understanding, these secret wounds. I knew when I got around to telling her, she would be the only one to understand what it is like to walk into your third-floor garden apartment, stairs creaking, and open the door to see your father on the sofa, holding in his lap a gurgling shisha and the neighborhood senorita you used to think was pretty, peering at you in the light of the naked lightbulb above his head, saying meet your new amma.

But she lives in Arizona? I asked.

And she sighed, her breath like the hiss of tire air escaping. She settled herself in her seat, rested her hands, nails painted bright red, on her knees, and said okay let's talk then.

Arizona is a promise, she said. A new life.

Someone lived there, but not her mother; *her mother* lived in Baltimore, a few houses down the street. Her mother was the helpful sort, the sort who cleans up messes, does what needs to be done. And I would have wondered what she meant except I sort of knew because that was what I imagined her to be like. She was always the one to bring in her husband's car for a wash, sitting on the chair and talking to me while I ran a washcloth over the tires. He is so busy, she would say, eyes sparking with love or something, and I would listen and wipe and make sure I pumped extra sprays of Juniper Breeze inside her car, because once she had said it reminded her of a forests and wouldn't it be nice to live in a cabin among the trees.

Who is someone? I asked.

And she smiled and said someone who understands me.

41

Is it a man? I asked, even though I knew that it was and also that the sudden chill in the car was not from the AC she was blasting directly at her face.

Her nose crinkled like she smelled something dead.

What was I, stupid? she asked. Besides, she didn't owe me a story.

She reached over and turned up the volume on the radio and sat back. We were both silent for a while. The way she held her neck all straight, I knew I had done something wrong. I had learned to fear stillness from my father. The back of my skull felt as if someone had slammed it against a doorway over and over, and I shook my head to dissolve the blurriness that was stinging at my eyes.

She had been the one who had smiled that brilliant, new-love smile at me, hadn't she, when I was sitting on the bench in the waiting area of the car wash, running my hands on the cold plastic, trying to forget the burn from the bruise my father had delivered to my face that very morning. She had sat down next to me and put her hand on my shoulder and told me to sparkle, sunshine, and asked me if I could keep a secret and that no one had to stay anywhere they didn't want to, and didn't I think that was amazing that you could just leave and that meant there was still a life out there for you. A different kind of life? And of course, it meant something, didn't it, the fact that she had known exactly what to say. We both wanted the same thing. Except, she wanted it with someone else.

She stared straight out the windshield and so did I, my heart racing faster than the road beneath us. On the radio, someone started singing to someone else called sweet Caroline. Flashes of conversations from the last three months were ripping through my head; I had imagined a moment like this so many times, in so many different ways, and all I could think of doing was holding her hand, feeling her warm palm against mine. Maybe if I touched her, the distance would disappear, maybe I could restore her to me.

Her hands were clasped between her knees. I wiped my palm against my leg, lifted my hand toward hers. She looked at me, her face a question. I froze, pretended I had been reaching for the volume knob on the radio all along. The silence returned. I had not imagined this was the way things would be between us. But they were. I could see it now.

Okay, then, I said, tell me what's in the box at least, and she said life, softly, her eyes slipping into liquid for a second, and then she slid her glasses back down to her nose and sighed and went back to her phone.

I had to wait to sneak a look in the trunk when we stopped for gas and pretend that I needed a spanner to tighten something in the engine. The box had all kinds of garbage: baby clothes, and envelopes, so many envelopes, all addressed to her. Ah, her name, her name. I ran my lips, my chin against the script, feeling the writing on my skin and wondered if she would feel as fluid in my hands as her name did in my mouth. A little brown album, hiding under everything, was full of pictures. Her looking like a child, eyes like sunshine, fresh, holding a red, screaming baby. The baby, older, on swings, in school. Her getting older, too. Then with a guy, his arms around both of them. Her short little life buried in plastic sleeves.

Hey, she called from the front. We gotta keep moving.

I shuffled the things around in the trunk. She was meant to be someone, something, to me. I knew it somewhere in the back of my head. I would have followed her anywhere, she must have known that too, must have known it was no accident I was always the one to wash her car. But here in my hands were these, her secrets, things I had hoped she would share with me. For all of a minute when she had entered the car, desperate with desire to get away, I had seen in the crinkle of her eyes the woman she must be with her husband, all scrapes and dents, tears and edges, the woman who needed me.

She said what are you doing back there, and I said nothing and shoved her stuff back in the back and headed to the front of the car with a hammer.

I thought you said you were going to get a spanner.

She was staring at me over the red-rimmed sunglasses, and I stumbled, my heart in my stomach suddenly, feeling like I had done something wrong.

I was looking for this, I said, and bent over the hood, wondering how long it would take her busy husband and helpful mother to realize she was gone. And the child. Would she listen for the front door to open every day, even knowing her mother was never coming back?

Okay, well let's hurry, she said.

I clanged around in the engine a little. My arms wanted to swing wildly, but I kept them close to me, thinking I should ask her to get out of the car, that she was on the wrong journey altogether. She wasn't even watching, probably thought she could trust me, that I knew what I was doing even though all I did was put a little dent in the carburetor. I pictured leaving her at the gas station, telling her to find her way home. But she wouldn't, would she? She could taste her new life already. And what if she cried? I had seen her cry before, her face like the world was lodged in her heart and exploding, and her shattering from the inside. My mother used to have the same face. You had to be a man, be strong, in front of a face like that. That was what my father taught me.

Be a man, always, he had said, and pushed my mother down the stairs, out the front door, telling her to leave, leave, never show her face again, that she was a bad mother because look at me sniveling, she was making a girl out of me. He was saving me from her, my father had said, holding me back from running to her crumpled at the front steps. That's what real men do.

I should have let her go, but I couldn't do it, could I, because she had leaned forward and was looking at herself in the little mirror above her seat, and from the little space between the hood and the dash all I could see was the slice of her flesh, the top of her breasts, starting to peek out of her pink shirt, a glitter-pink rhinestone in the middle. I couldn't send her out into the world, to the newness and to someone in Arizona. New things always get old, that I knew and even her, young and fresh, was already starting to decay on the inside. I could see it.

I closed the hood of the car and came back inside and started driving, and she could tell that something in my brain was working, and I could tell that she wanted to know what it was, but I smiled and I kept driving, and she just looked at me, eyes worried, fingers wrapped around her seat belt, and I wanted to say to her smile, love, smile. But I didn't. I kept driving and when the turnoff to the highway came, I kept driving some more, and she said where are you going. I said nothing, and just smiled, and kept going and she kept screaming and shouting and somewhere in there was rage and fear and some sort of disbelief, and I could see it all clearly, but there was nothing I could say to prepare her for what was coming, and so I kept driving, the metal tip of the hammer against my ankle, looking for the perfect spot.

ACKNOWLEDGMENTS

The author wishes to thank the editors of the journals in which these stories originally appeared:

Bartleby Snopes: "God in the chicken coop"

Concho River Review: "Sparkle, sunshine"

decomP Magazine: "To fix a broken thing" (as "smaller, lesser things")

Everyday Fiction: "Boxes that carry loneliness" (as "Boxes")

Gargoyle: "Listening for storms"

Hong Kong Review: "Wednesday"

Necessary Fiction: "First the heart, then the rest"

Nelle: "One more winter" (as "Winter Harvest in Lahore")

Pithead Chapel: "Lovebirds" (as "Lovebird")

Smokelong Quarterly: "Things I say to my son as he sleeps"

Waxwing: "Willow tree fever"

"Lovebirds" appeared in *Best Small Fictions 2021*, guest edited by Rion Amilcar Scott with series editor Nathan Leslie (Sonder Press). Thanks also to Wigleaf for naming the story to the *Wigleaf* Top 50 Very Short Fictions 2021.

ABOUT THE AUTHOR

Hananah Zaheer is a writer, editor, improvisor, and photographer. Born in Pakistan, she considers North Carolina home, and currently lives in Maryland with her husband and two boys.

Her writing has appeared in places such as *Kenyon Review*, *Best Small Fictions 2021*, *AGNI*, *Pithead Chapel*, *Smokelong*, *Virginia Quarterly Review*, *McSweeney's Internet Tendency*, *South West Review*, *Alaska Quarterly Review* (with a Notable Story mention in *Best American Short Stories 2019*), and *Michigan Quarterly Review*, where she won the Lawrence Foundation Prize for Fiction.

She serves as a fiction editor for *Los Angeles Review*, and as senior editor for *SAAG: a dissident literary anthology*, a project that seeks to make space for radical and experimental South Asian art and writing. She is the founder of the Dubai Literary Salon, an international prose-reading series.

This book was published with assistance from the Fall 2020 Literary Editing & Publishing class at the University of North Carolina at Chapel Hill. Contributing editors and designers were Elizabeth Bryan, Stephanie Harris, Ian Kennedy, Will Lowder, Carol Seigler, Samantha Shaw, Maia Sichitiu, and Anna-Lynn Wicker.